The True Nature of Technology

対訳

技術の正体

木田 元 著
Gen Kida

マイケル・エメリック 訳
Michael Emmerich

deco

The
True Nature
of
Technology

対話

技術の正体

木田 元 著
Gen Kida

マイケル・エメリック 訳
Michael Emmerich

deco

目次

•

はじめに
Prologue
4 / 5

技術の正体
The True Nature of Technology
44 / 45

春の旅立ち「風の色」
Spring Departures: "The Color of the Wind"
70 / 71

ふたたび廃墟に立って
Amidst the Ruins, Again
84 / 85

Translator's Afterword
訳者あとがき
88 / 89

ブックデザイン　寄藤文平+八田さつき(文平銀座)

はじめに
Prologue

・

はじめに

●

　「技術の正体」を書いたのは、もう二十二年も昔のことである。

　人間の理性が技術をつくったというのは実は間違いで、技術というものは理性よりももっと古い起源をもつ。したがって、人間が理性によって技術をコントロールできるというのはとんだ思いあがりではないか。要約すれば、そういうことを述べたものである。

　ありがたいことに、「技術の正体」は、高校の国語の教科書や大学の入学試験問題にたびたび採りあげられてきた。ごく短いものだが、高校生や予備校生だけでなく、多くの読者の関心を惹いたようで、私の書いた文章のなかでも、特に反響の大きいものの一つである。

　東日本大震災から三年たった今も、技術につ

Prologue

•

Already twenty-two years have passed since I wrote "The True Nature of Technology."

We are mistaken to think technology is a product of human reason, and in fact its origins can be traced back to an age that predates reason. We are getting above ourselves quite a lot when we tell ourselves human reason is capable of controlling technology. That, in a nutshell, is the argument I set out in this essay.

I have had the pleasure of seeing this piece be included in various high school textbooks for Japanese, and on university entrance exams. Short as it is, it seems to have interested not only students in high school and cram schools, but many others, too; it is one of the writings,

はじめに

いての私の考えは二十二年前と少しも変わっていない。むしろ、今度の大震災であらためて裏づけを与えられたような気さえしている。

　福島第一原発では、現在にいたるまで炉心の制御はもちろん、増えつづける汚染水の処理さえ満足にできていない。技術が人間のコントロール下から脱け出して、みずからの意思で動き、人間のほうがその部品と化してしまったかのようにさえ感じられる。これはもはや当事者の東京電力の怠慢だけを責めてすむ問題ではない。これだけ次から次へと事故が起きるということは、原子力発電という技術がもう人間の手

Prologue

•

among all I have published, that has attracted the most attention.

Three years after the Great East Japan Earthquake and Tsunami, my thinking on the subject of technology remains the same as it was twenty-two years ago. If anything, the disaster seems only to have lent further credence to my views.

To this day, not only has the core of the Fukushima Daiichi nuclear reactor not been brought under control, but no one has even come up with a satisfactory means of dealing with the ever-increasing quantities of radioactive water. One almost has the impression that

はじめに

に負えないところまできているからにちがいない。

　技術というものは、どうやら人間の思惑などには左右されず、自己運動し、自己展開するものらしい。技術は、技術者の前に多様な可能性を提示する。一方、技術者は、それを実現するとどうなるかといったことなど気にもとめず、ひたすらその実現をはかるだけなのだ。たとえ誰かがその実現をためらったとしても、かならず別の誰かがそれをやってのける。私には、人間は次から次へと可能性を広げていく技術の自己運動に、ただ酷使されているようにしか思われない。

　私がこうした技術観をもつようになったのには、ドイツの哲学者マルティン・ハイデガーの

Prologue

•

technology has broken free of human control and begun acting in accordance with its own will, and that we humans are merely a cog in its machinery. When things reach this point, you can't really put all the blame on Tokyo Electric for its negligence. The fact that accidents keep happening in quick succession demonstrates beyond any doubt that the technology used to produce nuclear energy has progressed until humans are no longer capable of managing it.

Technology is not, it seems, swayed by our intentions; it moves and develops on its own. Technology holds out to the expert a plethora of possibilities, and the expert strives only to make them real, heedless of the consequences.

はじめに

・

影響が大きい。ハイデガーがもし今生きていれば、「技術文明の自壊は、すでに始まっている」と言うだろう。ハイデガーは、晩年の講演で「アウシュビッツの能率的な大量虐殺と、収穫量だけを追求する今の農業は、まったく同じ原理に則（のっと）っている」と発言して、とんでもないことを言うと批判された。別に弁護するつもりもないが、ハイデガーが問題にしていたのは、非人間的な技術文明が、やがて天災や人災によって崩壊したあと、人類が真に覚醒（かくせい）する新しい時代が始まるかどうか、ということだったように思える。

　ハイデガーはナチスに加担したことで悪名を残したが、それは、アメリカやロシアはすでに技術の自己運動にとりこまれてしまっており、

Prologue

•

If one expert hesitates to make a technology practicable, someone else will come along and do so instead. From where I stand, it is all too apparent that we humans are being used by technology as it keeps enlarging its potentials.

I arrived at this view of technology in large part owing to the influence of the German philosopher Martin Heidegger. If Heidegger were alive today, I'm sure he would be telling us that the collapse of technological civilization has already begun. In a lecture he delivered near the end of his life, he observed that "agriculture is now a motorized food industry, the same thing in its essence as the production of corpses in the gas chambers and the extermination camps," for which he was

はじめに

・

　唯一ナチスだけが生きた自然を復権させることによって、非人間的な技術文明を乗り越える可能性を秘めていると考えたからのようだ。ところが、結局ナチスも列強の同類だということに気づき、その上ナチス内部の権力闘争にも敗れて、すべてに絶望したのだと弁明している。その後ハイデガーは、ひたすら技術の自壊を待ちつづけるというペシミスティックな姿勢に終始した。

　私は、技術だけでなく資本もまた一つの複雑系として自己運動をすると考えている。資本も、ある段階までは資本家や経営者や経済学者によってコントロールできると思われたのであろうが、やがて自己運動をはじめて、人間の手に負えなくなった。先のリーマン・ショックに

Prologue

•

roundly criticized. I have no intention of defending this statement, but I might note that the issue he seems to have been concerned with, ultimately, is whether, in the aftermath of the final destruction of an inhuman technological civilization by disasters either natural or manmade, humanity will arrive at a new, true awakening.

Heidegger has become infamous for his support of the Nazis. It appears, though, that his reason for doing so was that he saw the United States and Russia as being already in the grip of technology's self-driven operations, and thought only the Nazis could restore living nature to its rightful place, and thus overcome the inhumanity of technological civilization. He later tried to

はじめに

よる世界的な金融危機がその典型であろう。マルクスも、初期の『経済学・哲学草稿』においては、人間は資本を制御できるし、革命によって経済構造を変えることができると信じていた。しかし、晩年は、それはとても無理だと気づき、資本の自己運動の法則を追求しようと試みた。ハイデガーも「マルクスは歴史の本質的な次元に到達している」と高く評価している。

　ハイデガーや、彼の一世代上の哲学者ニーチェは、西洋文明そのものが行きづまっていると見て、新しい文化形成の可能性を模索した。
　西洋文明の基本的な考え方は、次のようなも

excuse himself by saying he eventually realized that the Nazis were really no different from the great powers, and that, after losing a power struggle within the party, he fell into a state of complete despair. For the rest of his life, Heidegger adopted a relentlessly pessimistic attitude, merely waiting for technology to destroy itself.

In my view, technology is not the only complex system that operates of its own accord: capital is just the same. Up to a point, no doubt, it seemed that capitalists, entrepreneurs, and economists were able to control capital, but then it began operating on its own, and humans could no longer make it do their bidding. The Lehman Shock and the global financial crisis it precipitated

はじめに

・

のである。神という超自然的な原理が設定され、自然というものは、その原理によって世界が制作される際の材料(マーテリア)にすぎない。哲学を含めて、ヨーロッパ文化は、明らかにこうした自然観を基底にして形成された。その帰結が巨大な技術文明であることは言うまでもない。

　ニーチェが生きた十九世紀末は、産業革命の時代だったこともあり、労働者が非人間的な労働を強いられるなど、技術文明の弊害が見えはじめていた。ニーチェは、超自然的な原理などはないとして、自然は世界を制作するための材料などではなく、植物が生長するように、生きて生成するものだと見ていた。事実、西洋においても、古代ギリシアのアナクシマンドロスやヘラクレイトスらいわゆる「ソクラテス以前の

stands as a perfect example of this. When he wrote his early *Economic and Philosophic Manuscripts*, Marx clearly thought that people could control capital, and that revolution could transform the economic structure. In his later years, he saw that this was impossible, and set about trying to pin down the rules by which capital operated instead. Heidegger held Marx in high regard, saying that he "reaches into an essential dimension of history."

Philosophers such as Heidegger and Nietzsche, who was active a generation earlier, believed Western civilization had arrived at a dead end, and started trying to grope their way toward

はじめに

　思想家たち」は、こうした自然観をいだいていた。ニーチェやハイデガーはそこに立ち返ろうとしていたのだ。

　こうした自然観は、われわれ日本人にもなじみ深いものである。古代日本人は、私たちが住む世界を「葦芽の如く萌え騰るものによりて成る」（古事記）と見、その力を「ムスヒ」（草ムス。苔ムス＋霊）と呼んでいた。日本人は、そうした力を秘めた母なる生きた自然に包みこまれ、それに順応して生きるのが人間の真のあり方だと、つい最近までそう信じて生きてきたのだ。

　私はこの数十年来、「反哲学」ということを提唱してきたが、それはニーチェやハイデガーが試みた哲学批判を日本人の立場で考えてみよ

Prologue

•

some new cultural form.

The core of Western thought can be summarized quite simply: God is taken to exist as a principle beyond nature, while nature is merely the *materia*—the material—from which that principle created the world. All European culture, including philosophy, is clearly rooted in this view of nature. It goes without saying that the vast technological civilization that came into being in Europe emerged a consequence of this view, this culture.

In the late nineteenth century, when Nietzsche lived, the terrible effects of technological civilization—the inhuman working conditions to which laborers were

はじめに

うとしたからである。生きた自然のなかでの技術のあり方は、どのようなものであろうか。ますます巨大化し、自己運動を起こしはじめた技術文明の前では、こうした思索ははかないものかもしれない。それでも私は、これを考えぬくことが自分の思想的課題だと思っている。

　東日本大震災では、大津波が沿岸の町々を次々と襲った。テレビでこの映像を最初に目にしたとき、「ああ、この光景、どこかで見たことがある」という強い既視感にとらわれた。あれこれ思い起こしているうちに、どこで見た光景なのかに思いあたった。どうやら第二次大戦

Prologue

•

subjected, for instance—were starting to be noticed, in part because the industrial revolution made them so obvious. Nietzsche saw nature not as mere material for the creation of the world, but as something that lived and developed, just like a plant as it grows. As it happens, the so-called pre-Socratic philosophers of Ancient Greece, including Anaximander and Heraclitus, had seen nature in the same way. Nietzsche and Heidegger were trying, that is, to return to that older position.

This vision of nature is something we are used to here in Japan. Ancient Japanese saw the world we inhabit as having "sprouted up like a reed" (*The Record of Ancient Matters*, 712), and

はじめに

•

敗戦の二か月ほどあとに見た、一面焼野原となった東京の情景らしい。十七歳になったばかりの私は、入学したての江田島の海軍兵学校を追い出され、その後ご厄介になっていた兵学校の教官の佐賀のご実家もおいとまし、放浪の旅に出たところだった。家族は満洲に残っていたので、どこにも私の帰るあてはなかった。九州から東京に向かって、何日も無蓋の貨物列車を乗り継いできたのだが、品川で降ろされて、途方に暮れて歩きまわっているうちに、あのあたりのどこかの高台から焼野原を眺めたのだろう。

あれから六十八年が経ち、日本も日本人もずいぶん変わった。朝鮮戦争やベトナム戦争といった、近隣の国の戦争に便乗して高度成長を達成し、経済的には繁栄し、ＧＤＰ（国内総生

Prologue

called the force of its growth musuhi. Until quite recently, Japanese believed that humans were meant to surrender themselves to the embrace of a motherly, living nature that was imbued with that force, and adapt themselves to it. That was the true way to live.

For the past few decades, I have been advocating what I call "anti-philosophy." I came to this notion because I wanted to think through the critiques that Nietzsche and Heidegger had leveled at philosophy, and to do so from my perspective as a Japanese. How should we view technology in the context of a living nature? Thinking of this sort may be all but powerless in the face of a relentlessly

はじめに

・

産）も世界第二位になった。それがまた、この大震災で振り出しにもどったような気がしてならない。

　ところが、震災後の日本は、あいかわらずなにかといえば経済成長ばかりをお題目に、株価の上下だけに一喜一憂している。目先のことばかりにとらわれすぎてはいないだろうか。震災後は、自然に対してもう少し謙虚な社会が設計されるかと期待したが、そうはならないようだ。政府のお金の使い方を見れば、謙虚さを失っていることがわかる。高度経済成長期に建設されたインフラの多くが耐用年限を迎えたり越えたりしているにもかかわらず、解体や補修といった金にならない事業には目を向けず、新たな公共事業を進めようとばかりしている。原発

Prologue

•

expanding technological civilization that is beginning to take control of itself, but still I feel this is my task as a thinker.

During the Great East Japan Earthquake and Tsunami, the tsunami washed over countless towns along the coast, one after the next. The first time I saw the images on television, I was seized by a powerful sense of déjà vu: *I've seen this before somewhere.* Casting my thoughts around, I suddenly realized what it was that I was remembering. It was the sight of Tokyo about two months after Japan's defeat in World War II, of a city that had been reduced to nothing but a vast expanse of charred rubble. I

はじめに

•

の危険さは十分にわかったはずなのに、はやくも停止中の原発の再稼動が議論されている。

　私たちは敗戦後、今から見れば信じられないような低い生活水準・経済水準のなかで不便な暮らしをしてきたが、別に卑屈(ひくつ)にもならなかったし、みじめな思いもしなかった。同胞(どうほう)を危険にさらしてまで、現在のような便利な生活を維持したいとは、私は思わない。ドアは自動でなくても手で開ければいいし、だれも使わないエスカレーターなど必要ない。こんなに自動車をつくりつづけなくてもよいし、無理して経済大国でありつづけなくてもよいと思うのだが、今の世の中を見ると、そう思わない人のほうが多いらしい。

　いつの世にも「時代の勢い」というものがあ

Prologue

•

had recently turned seventeen, and I had been kicked out of the Imperial Japanese Naval Academy on Etajima, even though I had only just started, and then I had left the house where I was staying in Saga—I had been taken in by the parents of one of my teachers at the Academy. Now I was just roaming the country. My family was still in Manchukuo, so I had no home to go back to. So I had set out from Kyushu to go to Tokyo, riding for days on a series of open-roofed cargo trains, and when I descended at Shinagawa I didn't know what to do, so I walked around, here and there, and that must have been when I saw that scene of utter destruction, from the top of some hill.

はじめに

るが、それに安易に同調したり、勝ち馬に乗ろうとしたりすると、とんでもないことになる。戦前、日本が国際連盟から脱退したとき、国民は拍手喝采した。ところが、これによって日本の国際的孤立は決定的になった。私が永年哲学を勉強してきて学んだのは、わからないのにわかったふりをするのがいちばんよくないということだった。世の大勢に流されず、立ち止まってよく疑い、よく考えることが必要なのではあるまいか。

　あの大地震の日は、突然の激しい揺れに驚いて、思わず家の前の公園に逃げ出した。みすぼ

Prologue

•

Sixty-eight years later, Japan and the Japanese have changed enormously. We achieved a period of remarkable growth, in part owing to the wars that were taking place in neighboring countries—the Korean War, the Vietnam War—and the economy flourished, increasing the country's GDP until it became the second highest in the world. I can't help feeling that the terrible disaster of 2011 had taken us back to the starting point.

And yet even after the disaster, Japan remains focused on economic growth, rejoicing and despairing over fluctuations in stock prices. Is it really right for us to concentrate so intently only on the things that are right in front of us? I had

はじめに

・

らしい老人が一人でうずくまっていたからか、若いお嬢さんが寄ってきて、「大丈夫ですか」と声をかけてくれた。ほっとして、「大丈夫だけど、大きな揺れだったね」などと応じながら、心のなかで「ああ、少し長く生きすぎたかな」と、先立っていった友人たちをほんのちょっと羨ましく思ったことを覚えている。

　テレビの伝える被災者たちの言動を見ていると、絶望のなかでもたがいを思いやり、隣人の安否を気づかっていた。どうやら私たち日本人にとっては、デカルトの言う「われ思う、ゆえにわれ在り」といったような意味での「われ」は存在しないし、そんな「われ」を確立したりする必要もなさそうだ。強いて言うなら、私たちのもとでは、「ひとを思いやり、ひととつな

Prologue

•

hoped that in the wake of the earthquake and tsunami we might set about building a society with a little more humility toward nature, but that doesn't seem to be happening. Looking at how the government is using money, you can see that if anything it has lost what humility it had. Much of the infrastructure Japan built during its period of rapid economic growth has either reached or passed the end of its useful life, but the government doesn't bother dismantling or repairing things—there is no profit there—choosing instead to move ahead with new public works. You'd think we would have realized by now just how dangerous nuclear energy is, but already the debate over whether

はじめに

がる、そこにこそわれの立ち現われる余地もある」とでもいったことになるのではあるまいか。

　この大災害から立ちなおる道は苦しく長いものになるだろう。老齢の私にできることなど、もうあまりない。本書には、「技術の正体」のほかに、若い人たちへのせめてものエールとして２つの短文を収録した。
　また本書には、それぞれ英訳も付した。美しい英語に翻訳してくれたマイケル・エメリックさんに感謝申し上げたい。技術文明をつくり上げた欧米先進国の方々、これから技術立国を目

or not to restart the stopped reactors has begun.

After the defeat, we Japanese lived lives filled with inconvenience, and had a standard of life so low and an economy so slow it is utterly unthinkable from a contemporary perspective. And yet we were neither abject nor miserable. I myself certainly have no desire to go on living with all the conveniences we now enjoy if doing so means exposing our brethren to danger. I don't need a door to open itself; I'll open it with my hand. We don't need empty escalators. We don't need to make so many cars, or to try so absurdly hard to hold onto our position an economic superpower. That is how I feel, at any rate—but as I look around me, it seems the

はじめに

•

指す開発途上国の方々にも読んでいただけたら幸いである。

2013 年 9 月
木田元

Prologue

•

majority doesn't see things the same way.

Every age has its own momentum, but if you let yourself fall in step with it too easily, or just try to make sure you're on the winning horse, you end up making awful mistakes. When Japan withdrew from the League of Nations before the war, the Japanese people applauded. But all this act did was cement Japan's isolation in the world. One of the things I have learned from studying philosophy all these years is that there is nothing worse than acting as though you understand something when you don't. It is crucial, I think, not to let yourself be swept along by the tide of the world—to stop, to doubt, and to think for yourself.

はじめに

・

Prologue

•

I was so shaken by the sudden, violent shaking when the earthquake came that without even thinking I ran out to the park in front of my house. A young woman—concerned, no doubt, to see a shabby-looking old man huddling there alone—came over and asked if I was all right. Relieved, I replied that I was, it was just that the swaying had been so strong. And yet at the same time, I recall thinking to myself that maybe I had lived a little too long, and feeling just a tiny bit jealous of my friends who have already passed on.

Watching those who were immediately affected by the catastrophe on television, I was

はじめに

・

Prologue

•

struck by the solicitude they showed each other even in the midst of despair, and by how concerned they were about their neighbors' safety. It seems we Japanese don't really possess the sort of "I" Descartes had in mind when he wrote, "I think, therefore I am," and I don't really see that we need to try and cultivate such a self. If anything, you might say of us: "Only through our compassion, through our ties to others, is each of us able to come into being as an I."

The path toward recovery from this enormous catastrophe will, no doubt, be arduous and long. There isn't much an old man like me can do to help. In this book, in addition to "The

はじめに

・

Prologue

•

True Nature of Technology," I have also included two short pieces that I hope might at least give encouragement to younger people.

The texts in this book have been presented alongside translations into English. I would like to thank Michael Emmerich for his beautiful translations. I truly hope this book will find readers among the citizens of the advanced nations of Europe and the United States, which first created our technological civilization, as well as in developing nations that are even now trying to use technology to gain a better place in the world.

Gen Kida

September 2013

技術の正体
The True Nature of Technology

技術の正体

　科学技術の発達はひたすら加速の度を高めている。半世紀前、私の子どもの頃のサイエンス・フィクションが百年後、二百年後の夢として描いてみせたことなど、とっくの昔に実現されてしまい、現実はそれをはるかに上まわってしまった。

　人類は今や本当に宇宙空間に居(きょ)を構えたし、核を分裂させたり融合させたりして巨大なエネルギーを引き出している。それは、一瞬の間に地球上の全生物を絶滅させうるほどのものである。試験管のなかで人間を誕生させ、動物の臓器を人間に移植し、遺伝子を組み換えて生物の新しい種をつくり出す。これらはすべて、かつては神の業(わざ)とされていたものである。今では人類はそれを、ほとんど日常茶飯(さはん)の事として引き

The True Nature of Technology

•

Technology progresses at an ever more rapid pace. Visions of how the world might look in a century or two that were elaborated in the science fiction of my childhood, fifty years ago, have long since become reality, and now reality has gone even further.

The human race has established a foothold in outer space, and we are using nuclear fission and fusion to draw tremendous quantities of energy from atoms—enough to extinguish every living thing on the planet in the blink of an eye. We create human lives in test tubes, transplant animal organs into human bodies, and genetically engineer new species. All these activities were once regarded as the prerogative

受けるまでになっている。

　こうした科学技術の発達がわれわれの生活を途方もなく便利にしてくれたことは確かである。食糧生産技術は大勢の人間を餓死から救ってくれ、医療技術は患者やその家族に光明をもたらしている。身のまわりを見まわしただけでも、どれだけわれわれが科学技術の恩恵に浴しているか、数え出したらきりもない。

　しかし、その同じ科学技術が地球の資源を枯渇させ、環境を破壊し、人類を絶えず絶滅の危険にさらしていることも、これまた言うまでもない。科学技術は明らかに両刃の剣なのであ

of the divine, and yet people have come to accept them as an almost ordinary part of the landscape of our lives.

There is no denying that such technological developments have made our daily existence extraordinarily convenient. Advances in food production have saved great numbers of people from starvation, while new medical techniques bring rays of hope to patients and their families. All you have to do is take a look around you and you will realize that we have benefitted from technology in more ways than you can count.

At the same time, it goes without saying that

る。果たして人間にはこの危険な武器を無事に使いこなしてゆく力があるのだろうか。

　もっとも、こうした危惧は今にはじまったことではない。二千五百年もの昔、すでにギリシアの悲劇詩人が、「不気味なものはさまざまにあるが、人間以上に不気味なものはない」と歌っている。人間は技術を駆使して、海を渡ってどこまでもゆくし、神々のなかでももっとも不朽なものだとされてきた大地をさえも飽くなく鋤きかえして疲れさせ、鳥や獣や魚を捕え、たくみに天災を避け病を癒すが、その技術が人間を善にも導けば悪にも導くからだ、というのである（ソフォクレス『アンチゴネー』）。となると、もっとも不気味なものとは、人間というよりも人間のもつ技術だということになろう。

those same technologies are exhausting the planet's resources, destroying the environment, and exposing humanity to the constant threat of annihilation. Technology is unambiguously a double-edged sword. The question is: are we capable enough to exploit the possibilities of this dangerous weapon we call technology without destroying ourselves in the process?

Of course, our sense of this danger is by no means a recent phenomenon. Two-and-a-half millennia ago, the Greek tragedian Sophocles had already written, in *Antigone*, "Numberless wonders, terrible wonders walk the world but none the match for man." Humankind exploits technology, Sophocles says, to travel great

しかし、そうした不気味な可能性を秘めてはいたにせよ、どの文化圏にもしかるべき生活技術はあって、それがいわば自然と協調しながら人間の暮らしを助けてきた。古代ギリシアにおいても、技術を意味する〈テクネー〉という言葉は、同時に芸術をも意味していたのであり、そうした技術＝芸術はむしろ自然の働きの一環、ないしはせいぜいそのちょっとした延長と受けとられていたのである。われわれの父祖が木を一本切りたおすにも祈りを捧げ、その木の命を生かすようにそれを削り、柱に立て屋根をかけ、雨露をしのいだそうした生活技術は、けっして自然を枯渇させ死滅させるようなものではなかったにちがいない。

　その技術が西洋と呼ばれる文化圏である時期

distances across the sea; he ceaselessly plows the earth—the oldest of all the gods, inexhaustible—until even it begins to tire; he catches birds and beasts and fish; he eludes disaster and cures disease. But while technology leads mankind to good, it also leads us to bad. Perhaps we might say, then, that the most terrible of wonders is less humanity itself than human technology.

And yet, while technology has always harbored terrible potentials, every culture developed its own technologies for living—things that helped people get along from one day to the next, but still remained in harmony with nature. The ancient Greek word for "technology," *techne*,

から異常に肥大しはじめ、悲劇詩人のあの危惧が現実のものとなってしまった。しかも、その異常に肥大した技術は、西洋という圏域を越えて、まるで癌細胞が全身を侵してゆくように、世界大の規模で増殖しはじめたのである。

　危険なものになってきたからというのでこれを放棄することなど、人類にはもうできそうにない。危険だと分かりながらもそれに頼るしかないのだが、その危険の水位はどんどん高まってゆくという抜きさしならない状況に、いま人類は置かれていることになる。

　こうした不気味なものに対処するうまい知恵など、私にもあるわけはない。ただ、私には、今日人類が直面しているこうした抜きさしならない事態を招いた原因の一つが、技術というも

The True Nature of Technology

•

also meant "art," and their notion of *techne* framed it as part of the natural world, or at most as a further development of nature. Our own ancestors used to offer up a prayer each time they chopped down a tree, then let it live on by stripping it of its bark, turning it into a pillar, and then putting a roof over it to gain shelter from the elements. Such everyday technologies seem unlikely ever to have exhausted nature, or destroyed it.

Then, somewhere along the way, in the cultural context known as "the West," technology began to grow beyond all proportion, and Sophocles's fears became reality. And then, over time, this bloated version of technology passed

のについてのわれわれのとんでもない思い違いにあるように思えてならないのである。

　われわれはこう教えられてきた。つまり、科学は人類の理性の産んだ偉大な叡智である。もともと科学は実用などとは無関係に、ひたすら物を冷静に見つめることから得られる無垢な知恵だったのである。それをたまたま実生活に応用したのが技術なのであり、その意味では技術も間接的には理性の所産である。人類の理性が産み出したものを、人類が理性によってコントロールできないはずはない。われわれ人類には、この程度のものを理性的にコントロールす

The True Nature of Technology

•

beyond the borders of the West, propagating itself on a global scale like cancer cells spreading through a body.

We know technology is dangerous. And yet the human race no longer seems capable of giving it up. We have no choice but to continue relying on it despite the risks, and so we find ourselves trapped in a situation that becomes ever more dangerous.

Obviously, I have no more insight into how we might deal with the wondrous terrors we confront than anyone else. I can't help thinking, though, that one reason we have landed in this helpless situation is that we have fallen pray to an outrageous misunderstanding of what

る力は十分あるはずだ、と。

　だが、本当にそうであろうか。

　人類の理性が科学を産み出し、その科学が技術を産み出したという、この順序に間違いはないのであろうか。しかし、ギリシアの詩人が不気味だと恐れていたのは、人類の理性の所産である科学技術などではなく、ただの技術である。科学が技術を産んだというのは間違いではないのか。むしろ、技術が異常に肥大してゆく過程で、あるいはその準備段階で科学を必要とし、いわばおのれの手先として科学を産み出したと考えるべきではないだろうか。

　そして、その技術にしても、人類がつくり出したというよりも、むしろ技術がはじめて人間を人間たらしめたのではなかろうか。原人類か

The True Nature of Technology

•

technology really is.

This is what we have been taught: that science is a great storehouse of wisdom born of human reason. In the beginning, they say, science was pure knowledge, unrelated to practical matters, derived from an intent, dispassionate attention to the things of this world. Technology arose when pure science found its way into everyday applications; and in this sense technology, too, is indirectly a product of reason. And of course, anything human reason has created must be susceptible of control by human reason. Surely it is within the human race's power to call on reason to master something so tame?

ら現生人類への発達過程を考えれば、そうとしか思えない。火を起こし、石器をつくり、衣服をととのえ、食物を保存する技術が、はじめて人間を人間に形成したにちがいないのだ。

　こうした技術に助けられて、その日暮らしの採集生活が可能だった熱帯・亜熱帯地方を離れ、寒冷な中緯度地帯に進出することのできた原人が、明日を生きるために今日から準備しておかねばならない生活のなかで、その時間意識にいわば過去や未来といった次元を開くことになり、こうしてはじめてホモ・サピエンスになりえたのだからである。

　私が問題にしたいのは、技術は人間が、あるいは人間の理性がつくり出したものだから、結局は人間が理性によってコントロールできるに

The True Nature of Technology

•

So we have been taught. But is this really true?

Could this narrative of progression—the idea that reason gave rise to science, and science gave rise to technology—be mistaken? The terrible wonder Sophocles feared was not, after all, this sort of *scientific* technology, born of human reason; he worried about technology itself. Perhaps the whole notion that science spawned technology is mistaken, and it is more accurate to say that as technology began to bloat beyond all reasonable proportion, or perhaps in the stages leading to that point, it came to require the aid of science, and so in fact it was technology that gave rise to science—a creature, as it were, that could do its

ちがいないという安易な、というより倨傲な考え方である。どうやら技術は理性などというものとは違った根源をもち、理性などよりももっと古い由来をもつものらしいのだから、理性などの手に負えるものではないと考えるべきなのである。

　たしかに技術が人間を助けてくれることは多い。もともと人間を人間にまでつくりあげてくれたものなのだから、それは当然であろう。だが、だからといって、技術の真意が分かったとか、技術が人間の意のままになるなどと思わない方がよい。技術の論理は人間とは異質なも

The True Nature of Technology

•

bidding.

We might make a similar observation concerning the birth of technology itself. It was not humans who created technology, but rather technology that made us human. This is really the only possibility when you consider the process by which primitive humans developed into their modern counterpart. The ability to create fire, to fashion stone implements and clothing, and to preserve foods is without doubt what first made humans human.

Such technologies enabled primitive humans to leave behind the tropical and subtropical regions where they had survived from day to day by hunting and gathering, and to advance

の、人間にとっては不気味なものだと考えて、畏敬(いけい)しながらもくれぐれも警戒を怠らない方がよいと思うのである。先ほど引いたギリシアの詩人は、すでに十分にそのことに気づいていたように思われる。

　技術のこの正体を見きわめることが、哲学のこれからの重要な課題になるであろうが、しかしそれは、これまでのように単に技術をいかにコントロールすべきかとか、科学知の論理と技術の論理の対比とか、技術と経済構造の関係を問うといったところにとどまってはなるまい。技術の人類史的な意味や、技術と芸術の同根性(どうこん)とその差異といったことをまでも根源的に問い、畏(おそ)れるものは畏れるだけの節度をわきまえたそうした技術論の展開が目指されねばならな

into the colder mid-latitudes, where it was necessary to prepare today in order to live through tomorrow. And this consciousness of time, which opened the door on whole new dimensions, on the past and the future, is what gave rise to Homo sapiens.

What I am trying to question here is the simplistic, arrogant notion that since technology was created by humans, or by human reason, reason must finally be capable of controlling it. It is more accurate to say, instead, that technology has its own origins, distinct from that of reason—that it appears, in fact, to be older than reason—and thus that it is beyond reason's power to control it.

いのである。

The True Nature of Technology

•

Technology helps us in all sorts of ways, it is true. Of course it does—it made us human in the first place, after all. But we should not let ourselves be deluded into thinking that this means we know where technology is headed, or that we can do with it whatever we please. We should tell ourselves that the logic of technology does not belong to the human realm; that it is a terrible wonder in the human world, something to be treated with awe, but also with unflagging caution. Sophocles, it seems, was already well aware of this.

Identifying the true nature of technology will, I'm sure, become an important theme for

技術の正体

・

philosophers. In order to achieve this, we must do more than simply consider how to control technology, or compare its logic to that of scientific knowledge, or think about how it relates to economic structures. We must ask fundamental questions about the meaning of technology as it pertains to the history of the human race, and ask what the fact that technology and art have the same origins suggests, and how they are different. We must strive toward a theory of technology rooted in an awareness that in this world certain things need to be treated with an appropriate degree of awe.

春の旅立ち「風の色」
Spring Departures:
"The Color of the Wind"

·

春の旅立ち「風の色」

・

　東北でも有数の豪雪地帯の一つに数えられる私の郷里のあたりでは、四月も半ば近くになってからの遅い春の訪れを、「風の色が変わった」という言い方で告げることがある。
　低く垂れこめた雲の下にひろがるモノクロームの雪景色に急に明るい陽が射しこみ、ぽっかりとのぞいた青空や、わずかに芽吹いた木々の新芽などによって鮮やかな色が注されると、たしかに風の色が変わったようにも感じられよう。
　「風光る」という俳句の季語があるが、それを生んだのと同じ感動が背景にありそうだ。
　この季節、進学や就職のために、そうした光る風のなかを大勢の若者たちが都会に旅立っていくにちがいない。

Spring Departures: "The Color of the Wind"

•

In my hometown, which stands in one of the snowiest regions in Northeast Japan, people note the arrival of spring—which comes somewhat late, toward the middle of April—by commenting that "the color of the wind has changed."

It's true. When the monochromatic expanse of snow is touched all at once by a burst of sunlight filtering through the low-hanging clouds, and the landscape is infused with color—a patch of blue sky yawning overhead, green shoots appearing on the trees—it really does feel as if the wind itself has taken on a different hue.

In haiku poetry, there is a seasonal term that

春の旅立ち「風の色」

●

　つい自分の郷里に近い東北の町々を思い浮かべてしまうのだが、殊にこの春、そのあたりから旅立っていく若者たちのうちには、まるで自分が大震災で傷ついた故郷の海や山、さらには家族や友人たちをさえ見捨てて逃げだそうとしているかのような、そんな後ろめたさを感じている人が多いのではなかろうか。

　そうした後ろめたい思いをともなった旅立ちということなら、私にも思い当たることがある。それも、やはり深く色づいた風のなかでの出発だった。

　もうはるか昔の話である。第二次大戦敗戦の四カ月ほど前、つまり一九四五年三月末のことだ。十六歳で旧制中学を卒業した私は、広島・江田島の海軍兵学校に入学するために、当時暮

Spring Departures: "The Color of the Wind"

•

means "the wind shines." That saying from my hometown draws, I suppose, on the same sense of joy that inspired this phrase.

This spring, too, as countless young men and women set out for the big cities to enroll in college or start a new job, the wind is surely shining all around them.

As I write these words, I find myself thinking of the towns close to my birthplace, in the Northeast. And it occurs to me that this spring, in particular, many of those youths who are departing for the cities are probably feeling guilty somehow, as if they are running away, abandoning the disaster-scarred shores and mountains of their hometowns, abandoning

らしていた満洲国（現・中国東北部）の新京（現・長春市）を旅立とうとしていた。

　一緒に入学する七人の同級生と共に、二日ほどかけて汽車で釜山（ふざん）まで南下し、下関（かん）行きの関釜（ぷ）連絡船で、物心ついて初めて日本に渡るのだ。

　新京駅には同行八人分の家族や友人が見送りにきてくれていた。そのとき別に私は、四カ月後に起こるソ連軍の侵攻や祖国の敗戦、戦後そこに残った者たちを襲う苛酷（かこく）な運命などを予感していたわけではないのに、自分が生きてふたたびこの街に帰ってくることはないだろうと妙に強く確信し、ある後ろめたさを感じていた。

　あの戦局では、むしろ軍籍に入る私の戦死する公算のほうがはるかに高かったのだが、それ

Spring Departures: "The Color of the Wind"

•

their families and friends.

I, too, have memories of the guilt that accompanies such departures. And I, too, set out on my journey at the same time of year, surrounded by a deeply colored wind.

This happened a very long time ago—about four months before Japan lost World War II, toward the end of March, 1945. I was sixteen, and I had just graduated from middle school in the old system; I would be leaving Hsinking (present-day Changchun) in Manchukuo (now the northeast of China), where my family lived then, to enroll in the Imperial Japanese Naval Academy on Etajima, in Hiroshima prefecture.

I would make the trip with seven classmates

春の旅立ち「風の色」

・

　でも自分は安全地帯に逃げ出そうとしているとどこかで思っていたのだろうか。

　三月末というこの季節、満洲は深い黄砂(こうさ)におおわれ、空も風もすべてが暗い黄土色に染まっていた。同じ春の旅立ちといっても、日本とはまるで違った色合いだ。

　結局、私は江田島で敗戦の日を迎え、家族は一年あまり後に満洲から引き揚げてきた。そして、満洲国の官吏(かんり)だったためシベリアに抑留(よくりゅう)された父も二年後に帰国し、一同無事に日本で再会できたのだが、それにしても、あの時感じたあの後ろめたさはなんだったのだろう。

　どうやら旅立ちといったものには、旅立つ自分は恵まれている、残る人たちに申しわけない、という意識がつきまとうものらしい。「後

who were enrolling in the Academy at the same time, riding the train south for two days to Pusan, and then taking the Kanpu Ferry to Shimonoseki. It was the first time since I was old enough to remember that I had ever made the crossing to Japan.

When our group of eight set off from Hsinking Station, our families and friends came to see us off. At the time, I had no way of foreseeing what would happen four months later: the Soviet invasion, the defeat of my home country, the harsh fate awaiting those who were left on the mainland after the war. And yet I felt an odd certainty that I would not be returning to this town, and this feeling inspired in me a kind of guilt.

ろめたさ」は、そうした意識にともなうぼんやりした感情ではないだろうか。

　そうだとすると、いま旅立とうとしている若い人たちにも、その後ろめたい気持ちをいつまでも忘れないでいてほしい、と言いたい気がする。

Spring Departures: "The Color of the Wind"

•

Given the direction the war had taken and my own enlistment in the navy, the likelihood that I was heading toward my death was extremely high, and yet evidently some part of me still felt as though I was running away, fleeing to a place of safety.

Late in March, Manchukuo was awash in dust that blew up from the deserts to the West: the sky and the wind coursing across it were dyed dark ochre. It was spring then, too, but the colors that surrounded me as I set out on that journey were utterly different from those that would have filled the air here in Japan.

As it happened, I was still on Etajima the day Japan was defeated. A year later, my family

春の旅立ち「風の色」

returned from Manchuria; my father, who was thrown into a labor camp in Siberia because he had been a government official in Manchukuo, came back two years later and we were all happily reunited in Japan. What, then, was that guilt I had felt when I left them?

Perhaps such guilt is just a part of every such embarkation: we feel fortunate to be setting out on a journey ourselves, and feel that we are betraying those we leave behind. The blurred sense of guilt we feel is a byproduct of that awareness.

Assuming that's true, I find myself wanting to tell all the young people embarking on their own journeys today to hold on to the guilt they feel, and never let themselves forget it.

ふたたび廃墟に立って
Amidst the Ruins, Again

ふたたび廃墟に立って

•

　第二次大戦敗戦のとき私は16歳、広島県の江田島にあった海軍兵学校の一年生だった。8月6日に広島への原爆投下を間近で目撃し、10日後に敗戦。父はシベリアに抑留(よくりゅう)され、家族は中国に残留していたので、私は一人で廃墟(はいきょ)となった戦後の日本に旅立ち、闇市(やみいち)で暮らしたり、農業の学校に入ったり、さんざん回り道をしたあげく、ロシアの作家ドストエフスキーに惹(ひ)かれ、結局は大学に入り直して哲学の道をあゆむことになった。

　いままた震災後の廃墟の映像を眼にし、82歳になった私にはもうなにもできそうもない

Amidst the Ruins, Again

•

I was sixteen when Japan was defeated in World War II, a freshman in the Imperial Japanese Naval Academy on the island of Etajima in Hiroshima prefecture. On August 6, I witnessed at close quarters the dropping of the atomic bomb on Hiroshima; ten days later, the war was lost. My father was sent to a labor camp in Siberia and the rest of my family was stranded in China, so I had to set out into the ruins of postwar Japan on my own, supporting myself by selling things on the black market, enrolling in a farming school, going down one path after another. Then, finally, having become fascinated by the Russian writer Dostoyevsky, I ended up going back to college and embarking on a

ふたたび廃墟に立って

・

が、かつてのあの旅立ちのころのことをまざまざと思い出している。あのころ、これ以上ないほど貧しかったが、なにも欲しくなかった。廃墟に立って、ただ自分が何者なのかを見きわめたいとだけ、烈(はげ)しく思っていたことを覚えている。

career as a philosopher.

When I see the images of the ruins this latest natural disaster has left in its wake, I realize that at the age of eighty-two there is nothing much I can do to contribute, and yet find myself besieged by memories of that period when I set out on my own journey into the ruins. I was as poor as poor can be then, but I wanted nothing. I was inspired, as I stood facing the ruins, only by the fierce desire to look hard at myself, and to see what was there.

Translator's Afterword

The tragedy that has come to be known as "3/11" in Japan, in a rather inappropriate analogy to 9/11, made many things clearer than anyone would ever have wanted them to be. A year or so after the earthquake, the tsunami,and the beginning of the nuclear disaster they triggered, I remember sitting at the dining table in my in-laws' house in Tokyo, my mind blank, drinking in the utter strangeness, the wondrous terror, of what had happened. Everything around me seemed just the same as always—children ambling past on the road outside, the wind rocking the branches of the maple in the yard, an ant zigzagging busily across the floor, tapping the wood with its feelers—and yet there was a blue Geiger counter on the table in front of me. I reached for it and switched it on, just to see what would happen, and it occurred to me that from the Geiger counter's perspective, there was no difference between

訳者あとがき

　9.11とのやや不適切な比較によって3.11と名付けられた悲劇は、誰もそこまで明確に思い知らされたくなかったことに、はっきりと生々しい輪郭を与えることになった。地震、津波、そしてそれらが引き起こした原発事故から一年後の二〇一二年。強い違和感、不気味さに呑まれながら、東京の妻の実家のダイニングテーブルに私は茫然と座っていた。こうしていると、なにひとつ変わっていないようだ。外の小道をのんびりと遊びながら歩く子供達、庭の夏紅葉の枝をゆらす風、触覚で木目を探りながら、床をあちこちと急いで渡る蟻一匹。しかし、同時にテーブル上には青いガイガーカウンターが置かれている。試してみようと、なんとなく手に取ってスイッチを入れてみる。そこで、ガイガーカウンターからすれば、天然の放射線も人工のそれもまったく同じだということに気がつく。

　災害というのは往々にして自然か人工のものかに区別される。しかし、3.11は私たちにこの領域の不可分さを

naturally occurring radiation and its artificially produced counterpart.

Disasters are often classified as either natural or human-made. Among the terrible truths to which 3/11 directed our attention was the final indivisibility of these two categories. The earthquake, the tsunami, and the nuclear meltdown were all part of the same dreadful event, the same sequence of cause and effect. Which is to say that the nuclear catastrophe was part of the broader natural disaster—that it was natural at the same time that it was human. It was, indeed, natural precisely because it was human, because it represented a failure of technology, and technology, as Kida Gen argues so powerfully in this essay, is a force of nature. Today, in this post-3/11 world, we need more than ever to reflect on this truth.

Michael Emmerich
September 2013

訳者あとがき

•

つきつけたのではないか。地震、津波、そして原発事故は一連の悲劇として繋がっており、原因と結果という延長線上に並んでいる。つまり、原発災害は大きな自然災害の一部であったという意味で、人間の事故でありながら、自然のなす業でもあった。突き詰めれば、人間による災害という意味でこそ自然だったのである。原発事故は科学技術の限界を象徴している。そもそも人間の技術とは、木田元氏が説くように、自然の所産であるのだから。3.11以降の世界で、今改めて木田氏の言葉を考えてみたい。

2013年9月

マイケル・エメリック

著者プロフィール

•

木田 元
Gen Kida

1928年山形県出身。哲学者。
東北大学哲学科卒業。中央大学名誉教授。
学生時代に習得したフランス語、ドイツ語、
ラテン語、古代ギリシア語の知識を背景に、
ハイデガー、フッサール、メルロ＝ポンティを
中心に現代西洋哲学の研究と翻訳を行なう。

哲学書
『現象学』(岩波新書)、『ハイデガーの思想』(岩波新書)
『メルロ＝ポンティの思想』(岩波書店)
『哲学と反哲学』(岩波書店)、『反哲学史』(講談社)
『反哲学入門』(新潮社) ほか

訳書
メルロ＝ポンティ『行動の構造』、『眼と精神』(みすず書房、共訳)
ハイデガー『シェリング講義』(新書館、共訳) ほか

エッセイ
『哲学以外』(みすず書房)、『闇屋になりそこねた哲学者』(晶文社)
『新人生論ノート』(集英社新書) ほか

訳者プロフィール

•

マイケル・エメリック
Michael Emmerich

1975年ニューヨーク生まれ。
翻訳家・日本文学研究者。
プリンストン大学を経て、
コロンビア大学大学院で日本文学の博士号を取得。
カリフォルニア大学ロサンゼルス校准教授。
よしもとばなな、川上弘美、古川日出男、
高橋源一郎、松浦理英子などの英訳を手がける。

訳書
よしもとばなな『ムーンライト・シャドウ』(朝日出版社) ほか

編著書
『Read Real Japanese Fiction』(Kodansha Amer inc.)
『Short Stories in Japanese』(Penguin Books) ほか

学術書
『The Tale of Genji : Translation,
Canonization, and World Literature』
(Columbia University Press) ほか

初出一覧

•

技術の正体

「正論」産経新聞社
1993年10月号。
木田元『哲学以外』
みすず書房(1997年)再録。

•

春の旅立ち「風の色」

「朝日新聞」
2012年4月3日。

•

ふたたび廃墟に立って

河合塾
『「東日本大震災」
復興と学び 応援プロジェクト』2011年。

対訳　技術の正体
The True Nature of Technology

2013年11月28日　初版第1刷発行

著者　木田元

訳者　マイケル・エメリック

発行者　髙橋団吉
発行所　株式会社デコ
〒101-0051
東京都千代田区神田神保町1-64
神保町協和ビル2階
☎ 03-6273-7781(編集)・7782(販売)
http://www.deco-net.com/
印刷所　新日本印刷株式会社
DTP　ステーションS
編集　大塚真(デコ)

©2013　Gen Kida, Michael Emmerich　Printed in Japan
ISBN978-4-906905-07-2 C0010

デコの本

あさって歯医者さんに行こう　高橋順子	1400円
この海に　高橋順子 / J・M・シング 原作	1400円
月の名前　高橋順子 文 / 佐藤秀明 写真	2500円
眠って生きろ　鳥越俊太郎・塩見利明	1200円
健康半分　赤瀬川原平	1200円
スマートメディア 新聞・テレビ・雑誌の次のかたちを考える　中村滋	1200円
自由訳 方丈記　新井満	1400円
ぼくらの昆虫採集　養老孟司・奥本大三郎・池田清彦　監修	2800円
大昆虫博公式ガイドブック すごい虫131 養老孟司・奥本大三郎・池田清彦　監修	1400円
虫と遊ぶ12か月　奥山英治	2500円
完全女子版! 自転車メンテナンスブック 山田麻千子・中里景一　監修	1400円
うちこハローノート　DECO 編	600円
加藤嶺夫写真全集 昭和の東京1 新宿区 加藤嶺夫写真全集 昭和の東京2 台東区 加藤嶺夫写真全集 昭和の東京3 千代田区 川本三郎・泉麻人　監修	各1800円

価格はすべて税別です